First published in 2007 by
Franklin Watts
338 Euston Road
London
NW1 3BH

Franklin Watts Australia
Level 17 / 207 Kent Street
Sydney
NSW 2000

A CIP catalogue record for this book is available from the British Library.

ISBN 978 0 7496 7144 0 (hbk)
ISBN 978 0 7496 7703 9 (pbk)

Series Editor: Jackie Hamley
Series Advisors: Dr Barrie Wade, Dr Hilary Minns
Series Designer: Peter Scoulding

Printed in China

Franklin Watts is a division of
Hachette Children's Books,
an Hachette Livre UK company.

READING CORNER

Spilt Milk

Written by
Anne Adeney

Illustrated by
Stephen Holmes

W
FRANKLIN WATTS
LONDON • SYDNEY

Anne Adeney

"I always looked forward to my children being old enough to stop spilling things. But now they are teenagers and I still change the tablecloth every day!"

Stephen Holmes

"When I was a boy, I wanted to be an astronaut, and to paint pictures of animals. Now I've painted lots of animals. So I suppose it's off to the moon next!"

This is the milk
that Jack spilt.

This is Simba,
who drank the milk
that Jack spilt.

This is Grandpa,
who fell over Simba,

who drank the milk
that Jack spilt.

These are the false teeth
that shot out of Grandpa ...

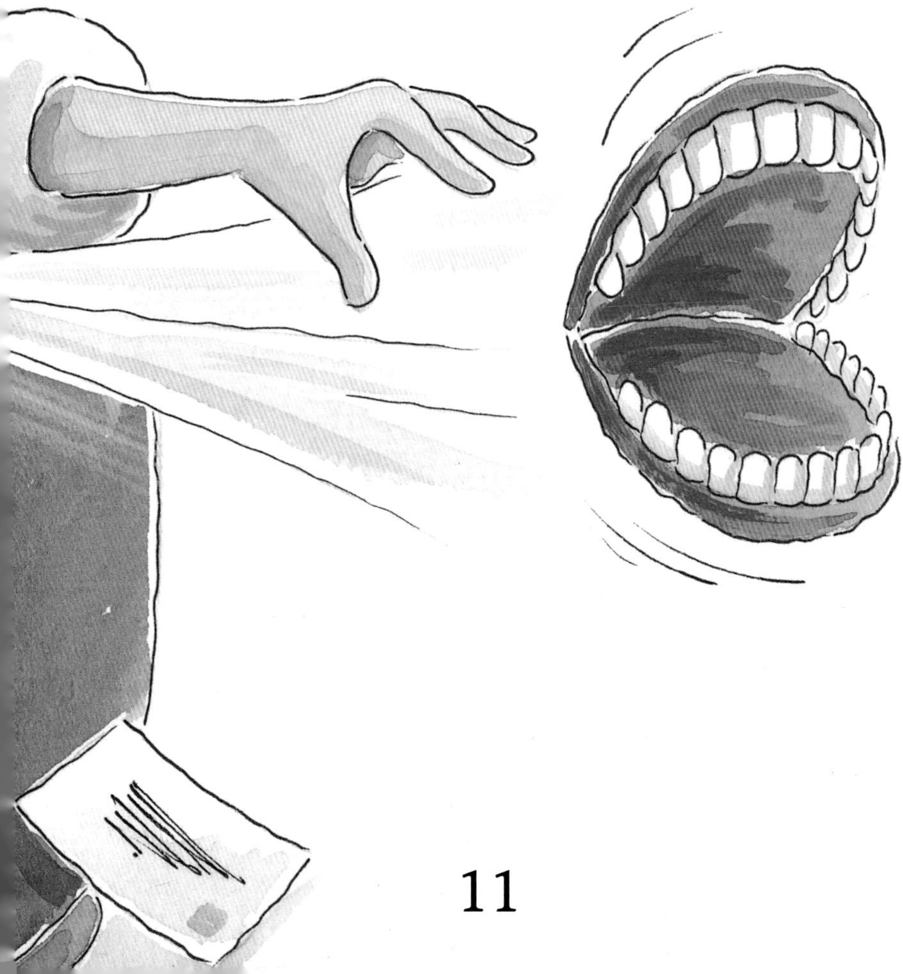

... who fell over Simba,
who drank the milk
that Jack spilt.

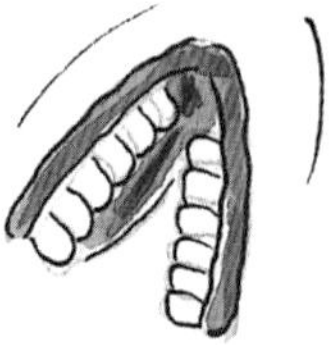

This is Spot,
who caught the false teeth
that shot out of Grandpa ...

... who fell over Simba,
who drank the milk
that Jack spilt.

This is Dad,
who grabbed the false teeth
that shot out of Grandpa ...

... who fell over Simba,
who drank the milk
that Jack spilt.

This is the milk
that Dad spilt!

Notes for parents and teachers

READING CORNER has been structured to provide maximum support for new readers. The stories may be used by adults for sharing with young children. Primarily, however, the stories are designed for newly independent readers, whether they are reading these books in bed at night, or in the reading corner at school or in the library.

Starting to read alone can be a daunting prospect. READING CORNER helps by providing visual support and repeating words and phrases, while making reading enjoyable. These books will develop confidence in the new reader, and encourage a love of reading that will last a lifetime!

If you are reading this book with a child, here are a few tips:

1. Talk about the story before you start reading. Look at the cover and the title. What might the story be about? Why might the child like it?

2. Encourage the child to reread the story, and to retell the story in their own words, using the illustrations to remind them what has happened.

3. Discuss the story and see if the child can relate it to their own experience, or perhaps compare it to another story they know.

4. Give praise! Small mistakes need not always be corrected.

READING CORNER covers three grades of early reading ability, with three levels at each grade. Each level has a certain number of words per story, indicated by the number of bars on the spine of the book, to allow you to choose the right book for a young reader:

GRADE 1	GRADE 2	GRADE 3
50 words	130 words	250 words
70 words	160 words	350 words
100 words	200 words	450 words